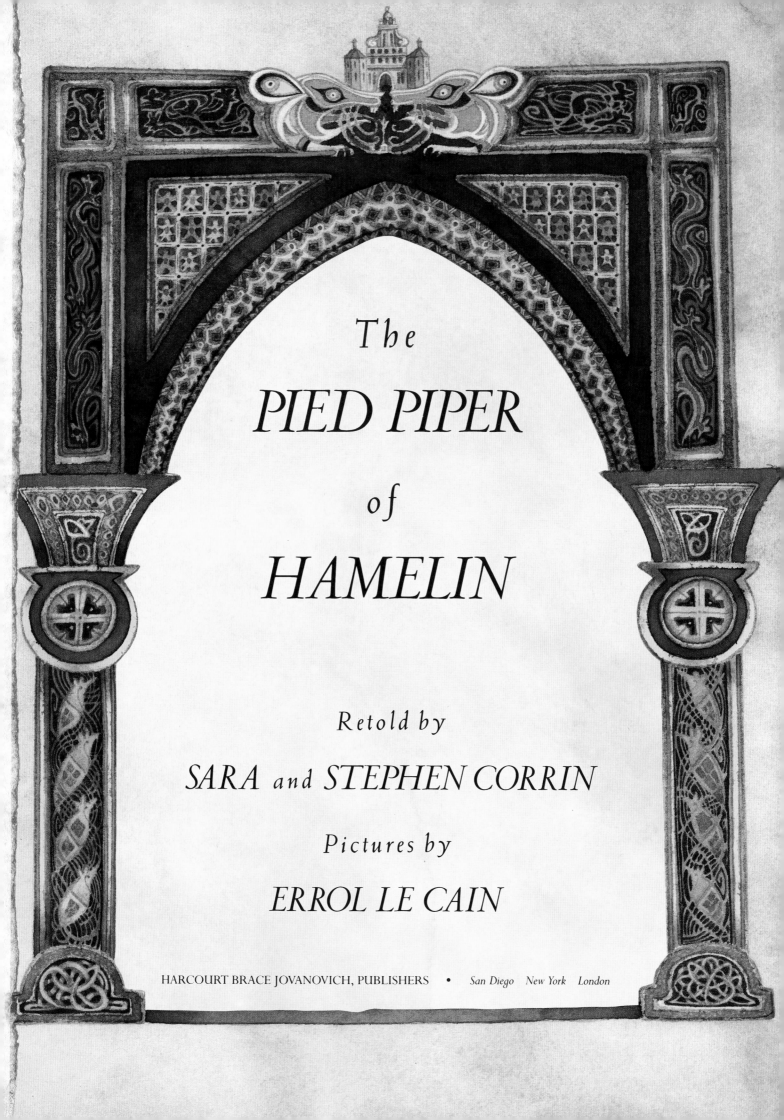

The
PIED PIPER
of
HAMELIN

Retold by

SARA and *STEPHEN CORRIN*

Pictures by

ERROL LE CAIN

HARCOURT BRACE JOVANOVICH, PUBLISHERS • San Diego New York London

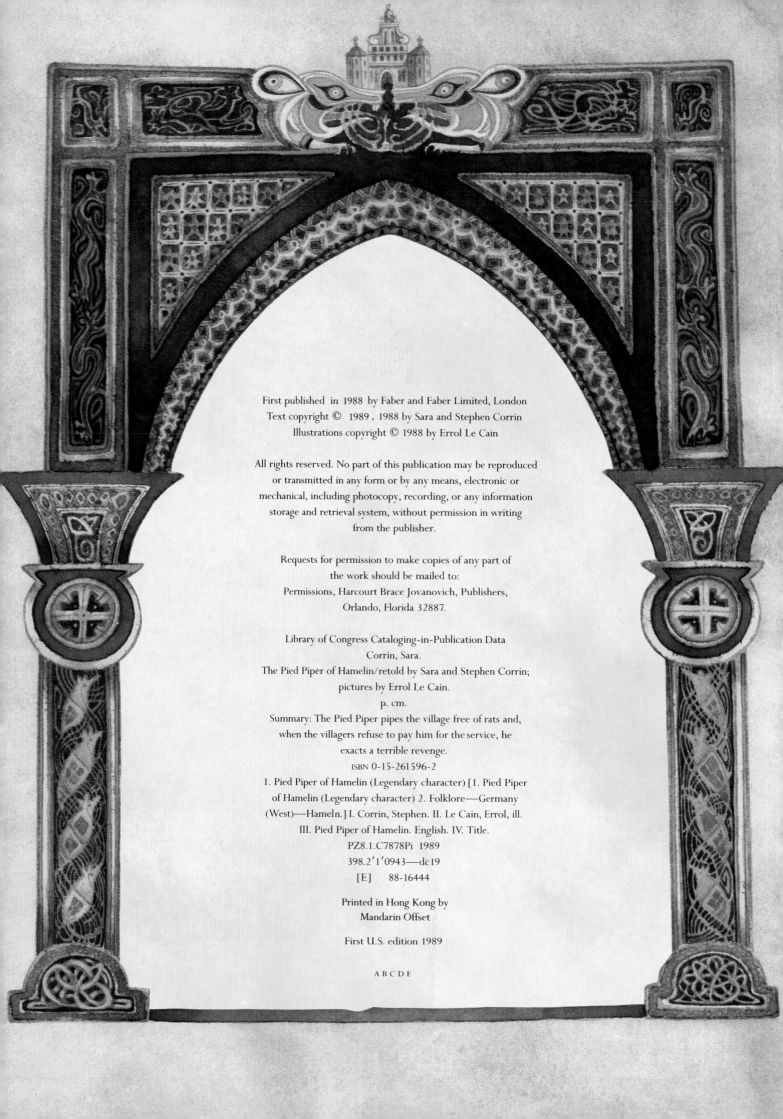

First published in 1988 by Faber and Faber Limited, London
Text copyright © 1989 , 1988 by Sara and Stephen Corrin
Illustrations copyright © 1988 by Errol Le Cain

Requests for permission to make copies of any part of
the work should be mailed to:
Permissions, Harcourt Brace Jovanovich, Publishers,
Orlando, Florida 32887.

Library of Congress Cataloging-in-Publication Data
Corrin, Sara.
The Pied Piper of Hamelin/retold by Sara and Stephen Corrin;
pictures by Errol Le Cain.
p. cm.
Summary: The Pied Piper pipes the village free of rats and,
when the villagers refuse to pay him for the service, he
exacts a terrible revenge.
ISBN 0-15-261596-2
1. Pied Piper of Hamelin (Legendary character) [1. Pied Piper
of Hamelin (Legendary character) 2. Folklore—Germany
(West)—Hameln.] I. Corrin, Stephen. II. Le Cain, Errol, ill.
III. Pied Piper of Hamelin. English. IV. Title.
PZ8.1.C7878Pi 1989
398.2′1′0943—dc19
[E]   88-16444

Printed in Hong Kong by
Mandarin Offset

First U.S. edition 1989

A B C D E

for Phyllis Hunt
with love and gratitude

Sara and Stephen Corrin, and Errol Le Cain

The town of Hamelin was a pretty little place, with narrow streets and overhanging gables that all but met above the heads of the passers-by. It was prosperous, too, for it was a trading town and the warehouses that stood along the River Weser were crammed with grain. Perhaps that was the trouble, for the town was infested with rats.

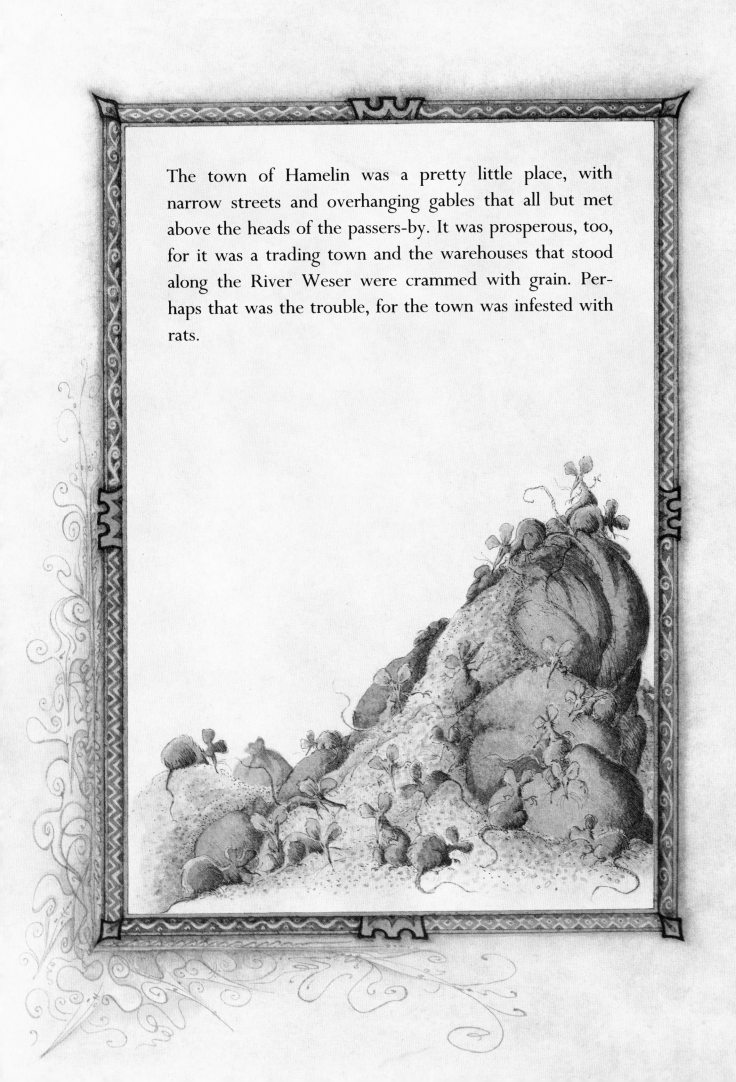

They turned up everywhere. Wherever you looked, beady, mocking eyes blinked up at you and long, skinny tails tickled your feet as the rats flashed past. They tripped you as you made your way upstairs and nipped at your fingers as you held on to the banisters. They burrowed into bonnets, nested in boots and shoes, and even set up house in grandfather clocks. They crept under blankets, tore into pillows, and wrapped themselves in sheets.

They even nibbled at the decorative trim of cradles, and no sooner would a watchful mother shoo three rats away than six more would be there. Their shrieking and squeaking drowned every other noise, so that the people of Hamelin could hardly hear each other speak.

The mill where the corn was produced was their favorite haunt, but the rats weren't terribly choosy about where they went or whom they honored with their visits. It was in the kitchens that they wreaked the greatest havoc. Cheeses disappeared from vats, kegs of herrings were split open, and tureens of soup were licked clean. If a cook tried to make bread a rat would peer over the rim of the mixing bowl, and when it was finally baked the rats usually managed to eat every last crumb before it could reach the table.

After months of this sort of thing, the citizens of Hamelin were hungry and furious. Some blamed the millers, for it was their storehouses that attracted the pests to the town. The millers in turn blamed the people who demanded corn for their bread. Husbands blamed wives for producing the mouth-watering odors that lured the rats to their kitchens and wives blamed husbands for insisting on the roasts and cakes they were accustomed to.

But when it came to pinning the blame on one single culprit, the people of Hamelin turned one and all on the Mayor. For the Mayor and his councillors were doing nothing about it. They couldn't think of anything *to* do.

So the citizens marched in procession to the Town Hall. They banged on the door. The doorkeeper peeped out and told them that the Mayor was in council and far too busy to see them, but the townspeople refused to be put off.

"We shall not—*not*—go away until we've seen him," they shouted. And they kept on screaming and yelling until finally, after three hours, the Mayor appeared on his balcony. He was a round, fat man and usually seemed very pleased with himself; when he wore his official Mayor's regalia, he simply swelled with a sense of his own importance. But today he looked timid and sheepish, despite his robes of office.

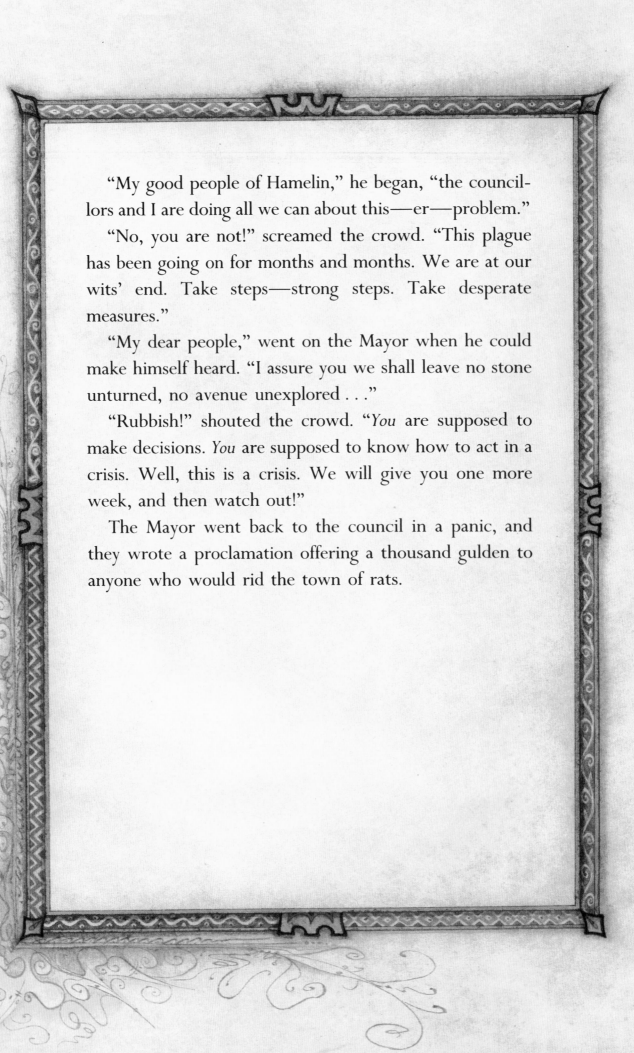

"My good people of Hamelin," he began, "the councillors and I are doing all we can about this—er—problem."

"No, you are not!" screamed the crowd. "This plague has been going on for months and months. We are at our wits' end. Take steps—strong steps. Take desperate measures."

"My dear people," went on the Mayor when he could make himself heard. "I assure you we shall leave no stone unturned, no avenue unexplored . . ."

"Rubbish!" shouted the crowd. "*You* are supposed to make decisions. *You* are supposed to know how to act in a crisis. Well, this is a crisis. We will give you one more week, and then watch out!"

The Mayor went back to the council in a panic, and they wrote a proclamation offering a thousand gulden to anyone who would rid the town of rats.

The next afternoon a handsome yet strange-looking fellow appeared in Hamelin. He was wearing a costume of many colors and a red and yellow scarf, with a pipe dangling from the end, around his neck. He went straight to the Town Hall and asked to see the Mayor.

"What is your business?" asked the doorkeeper suspiciously.

"Just tell him this," said the stranger. "I am a rat-catcher by trade and

I can rid this town of all the rats."

The doorkeeper rushed off to speak to the Mayor and came quickly back to show the stranger into the council chamber.

"What is this?" said the Mayor. "Do you claim to be able to rid the town of rats?"

"I do," replied the stranger. "I have a charm by which I can draw all harmful creatures after me. Last winter I freed the great Cham of Tartary of a plague of lice, and in the spring I delivered the Nizam of Asia from a monstrous brood of vampire bats. Now, if your Honors will give me a thousand gulden I will free *your* town of vermin."

"ONE THOUSAND?" exclaimed the councillors in chorus. "We'll give you FIFTY THOUSAND!"

The stranger smiled and turned toward the door. He was halfway there when the Mayor called, "What is your name?"

He looked back and smiled again. "People call me the Pied Piper," he said and then was gone.

Down in the street the Piper's keen green eyes twinkled as he pursed his lips ready to begin his tune. He had played only three notes when a most sinister sound began to rise from the ground like the rumblings of some vast crowd. As it rose louder and louder thousands of rats came scurrying into the streets to follow the Piper as he played his magical tune. From narrow street to narrow street, through tiny alleys, twisty slopes, down rickety steps and steep passageways they followed him until they came to the river. Then the Piper dipped one foot into the water and every single rat plunged into the fast-flowing river. They plunged in and drowned—all except one, who managed to swim to the other side to warn all other rats never to set foot in Hamelin again.

Can you imagine the joy of the people of Hamelin when they discovered there were no more rats in their houses? No, you can't, for it was beyond belief. They rang the church bells and sang and danced in the streets, while the Mayor issued a proclamation ordering all nests and rat-holes to be blocked up.

In the midst of all the rejoicing and frantic activity the Piper appeared in the marketplace, as if from nowhere, and placed himself in front of the Mayor.

"My thousand gulden, if you please," was all he said.

"A thousand gulden!" exclaimed the Mayor.

"A thousand gulden!" repeated the councillors.

Why, they thought, even half that sum would keep them in roast beef and fine wine for many months. Why pay all that money to this odd fellow just for playing a tune on his pipe?

"Come, come, my man," said the Mayor with a leer. "All those rats were drowned in the river; we saw it with our own eyes. What is dead can never return. When we said a thousand gulden we were joking. But no one can say we're mean here in Hamelin. We'll give you fifty gulden. Isn't that generous?"

"I have no time to waste," said the Piper scornfully. "I have kept my part of the bargain. Now you are honor-bound to keep yours. I have promised to be with the Caliph in Baghdad by dinnertime tomorrow to rid him of a plague of scorpions. Pay up—or you will hear me play a tune of a different kind."

"I'll not bandy words with a piper," said the Mayor. "Do you dare to threaten us, you insolent rogue? You can play your pipe till kingdom come for all we care."

Word soon spread that the Piper had insisted on his thousand gulden and the Mayor had refused to pay. The people of Hamelin, to their eternal shame, took the Mayor's side against the Piper.

"He's a sorcerer," they said. "He may be the devil himself! He's not going to get our precious money just for playing a tune."

The Piper looked at them with contempt and turned away. No one saw where he went, but the next morning he was back. It was June 26th, the Feast of St. John and St. Paul, and all the adults were in church. The Piper was dressed like a hunter, with a hat of the most brilliant red, and there was a frightening gleam in his steely green eyes. He put his pipe to his lips, and he had played only three notes when there was a stirring in every house in Hamelin. Boys and girls came pouring out—the Mayor's own daughter among them—chattering and jostling and running after him as he played his enchanting tune.

Can you imagine how the Mayor and his councillors and all the townspeople felt as they came out of church? They stood stock-still, every single one of them, unable to move for sheer horror, while their children skipped down the High Street after the Piper to the river bank, just as the rats had done. But when the Piper reached the river he suddenly turned toward the hill called the Koppenberg, and the people sighed with relief.

"He can never cross that great hill," they said. "He's bound to stop now."

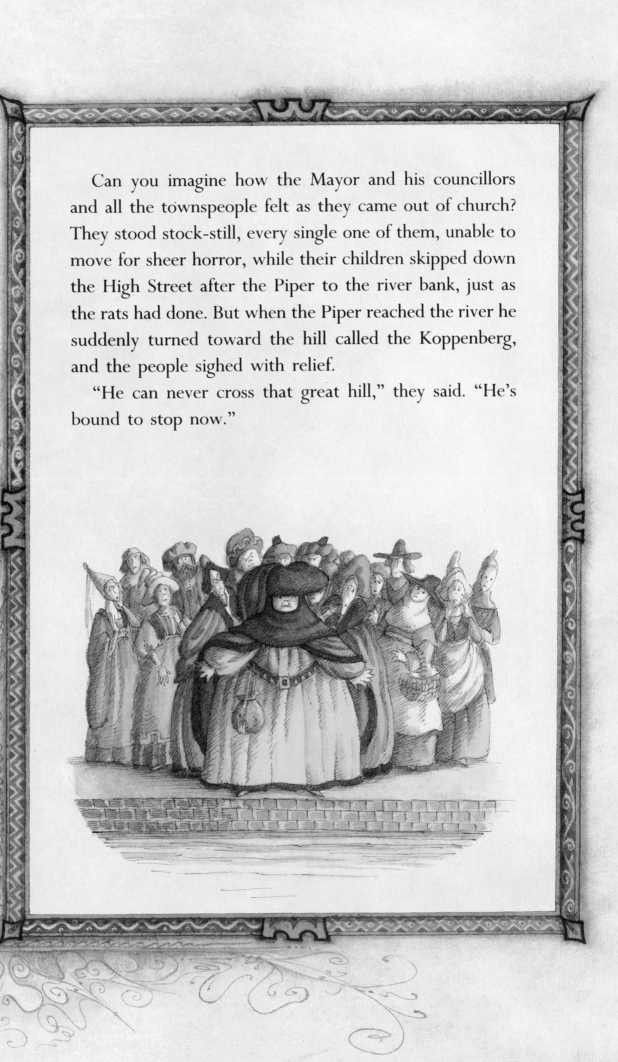

But they were wrong. For when he reached the mountainside

a little door opened

and in went the Piper with the children after him, every single one—except one lame boy who reached the door just as it closed. With the Piper and the rest of the children vanished, the Mayor and his councillors were left to face the fury of the citizens.

The Mayor did all he could. He sent out messengers north, south, east, and west to find the Piper and offer him any sum of money he asked if only he would bring the children back. But the messengers returned one after another, after many days of searching, with nothing to report. They had found no trace of the Piper anywhere.

In every home in Hamelin there was weeping and mourning and in the Mayor's home, too, for thanks to his greed he had lost his own daughter. He shut himself up in his house for fourteen days, not daring to show his face, and when he ventured out again he was barely recognizable. He issued an order that the name of the street where the children had last been seen should be changed to *Bungenlosenstrasse*, which means "the street without a drum," and that no drum or music of any kind was ever to be played there, not even when a bride and bridegroom walked it after their wedding. And he had the whole sad tale carved

in stone on the main buildings of the town for all to read and remember. It may be seen there to this very day.

The lame boy who was left behind said that the Piper had promised to take the children to a country of marvels where they would live happily forever and his lame leg would be cured. But could the Piper be believed? Or had he led the children by an underground passage to some distant land beyond the mountains?

Whatever the truth, they never returned, and for many years the people of Hamelin dated all events in their town from that terrible day in 1284 when their children were lost forever.

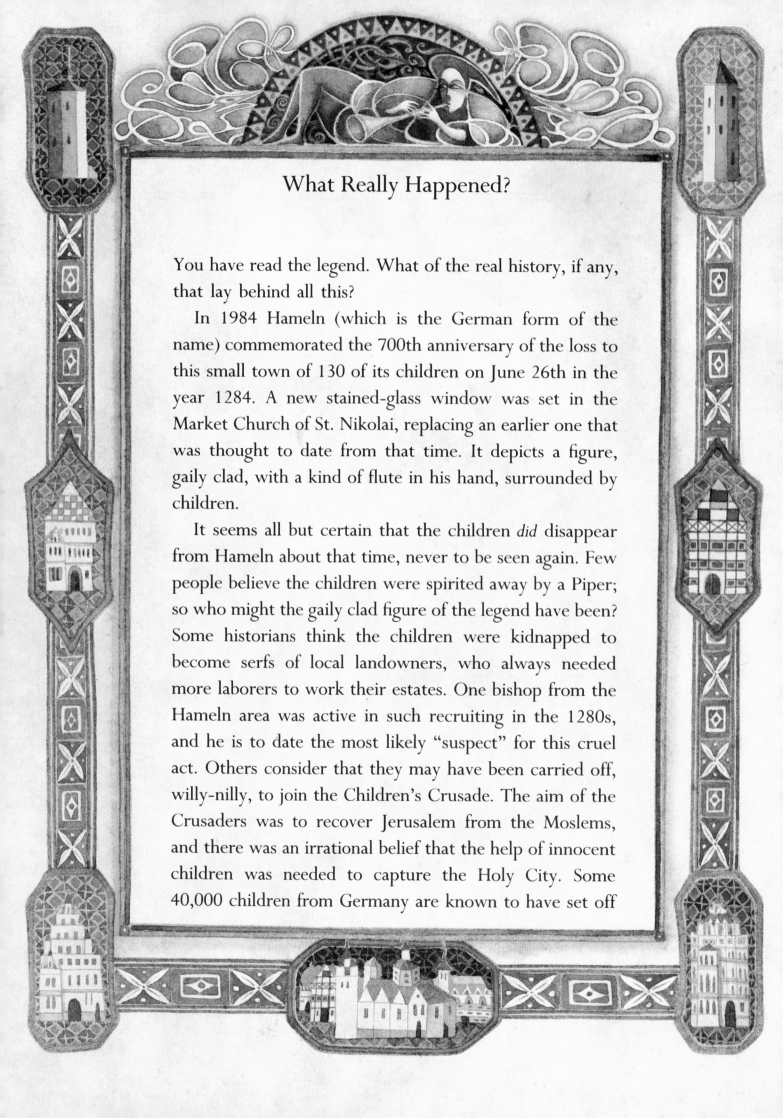

What Really Happened?

You have read the legend. What of the real history, if any, that lay behind all this?

In 1984 Hameln (which is the German form of the name) commemorated the 700th anniversary of the loss to this small town of 130 of its children on June 26th in the year 1284. A new stained-glass window was set in the Market Church of St. Nikolai, replacing an earlier one that was thought to date from that time. It depicts a figure, gaily clad, with a kind of flute in his hand, surrounded by children.

It seems all but certain that the children *did* disappear from Hameln about that time, never to be seen again. Few people believe the children were spirited away by a Piper; so who might the gaily clad figure of the legend have been? Some historians think the children were kidnapped to become serfs of local landowners, who always needed more laborers to work their estates. One bishop from the Hameln area was active in such recruiting in the 1280s, and he is to date the most likely "suspect" for this cruel act. Others consider that they may have been carried off, willy-nilly, to join the Children's Crusade. The aim of the Crusaders was to recover Jerusalem from the Moslems, and there was an irrational belief that the help of innocent children was needed to capture the Holy City. Some 40,000 children from Germany are known to have set off

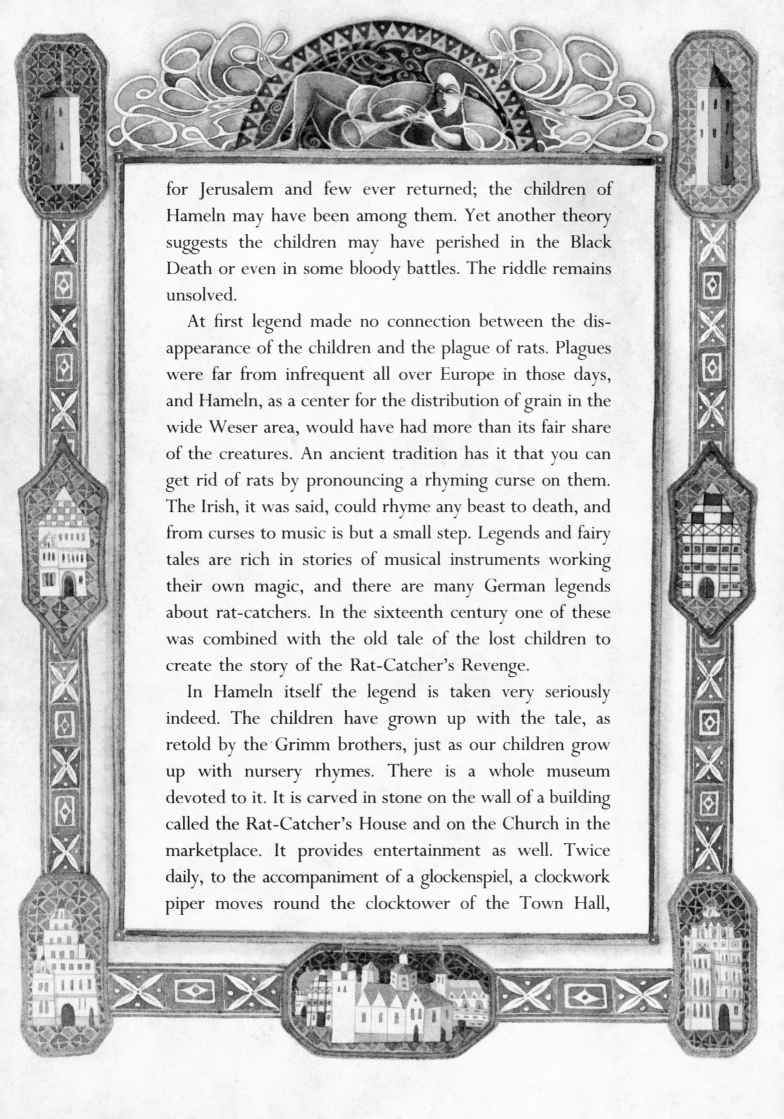

for Jerusalem and few ever returned; the children of Hameln may have been among them. Yet another theory suggests the children may have perished in the Black Death or even in some bloody battles. The riddle remains unsolved.

At first legend made no connection between the disappearance of the children and the plague of rats. Plagues were far from infrequent all over Europe in those days, and Hameln, as a center for the distribution of grain in the wide Weser area, would have had more than its fair share of the creatures. An ancient tradition has it that you can get rid of rats by pronouncing a rhyming curse on them. The Irish, it was said, could rhyme any beast to death, and from curses to music is but a small step. Legends and fairy tales are rich in stories of musical instruments working their own magic, and there are many German legends about rat-catchers. In the sixteenth century one of these was combined with the old tale of the lost children to create the story of the Rat-Catcher's Revenge.

In Hameln itself the legend is taken very seriously indeed. The children have grown up with the tale, as retold by the Grimm brothers, just as our children grow up with nursery rhymes. There is a whole museum devoted to it. It is carved in stone on the wall of a building called the Rat-Catcher's House and on the Church in the marketplace. It provides entertainment as well. Twice daily, to the accompaniment of a glockenspiel, a clockwork piper moves round the clocktower of the Town Hall,

followed by clockwork rats and children, and every week throughout the summer the tale is told in colorful musical pageantry in the main square. Everywhere in shops, restaurants, schools, and houses the Piper and his followers are depicted in wood carvings, in iron and metalwork, in beautiful bronzes and patterns of silk.

The story has become famous all over the world in many versions. It has been presented in opera, ballet, and film, in plays and in poems. In Germany it is best known through the Grimm tale of "The Rat-Catcher," but for English-speaking children the best version of all is Browning's brilliant poem "The Pied Piper of Hamelin."